# Boy, You're Amazing!

## Virginia Kroll

ILLUSTRATED BY
## Sachiko Yoshikawa

Albert Whitman & Company, Morton Grove, Illinois

With love to David (wonderful husband);
Seth, Josh, and Noah (sensational sons);
and dear friends Jack Edson (artist), Steve Cavallo (teacher),
Paul Bloom (guidance counselor), Rev. Randy Johnson (minister),
and Fr. Walter Grabowski (priest)—boys, you're amazing!—V.K.

To my wild brothers-in-law, Tom and Dean.—S.Y.

The illustrator would like to give special thanks to
Namiko Rudi, Kana Suzuki, and Charlie Whitesell.

Library of Congress Cataloging-in-Publication Data

Kroll, Virginia L.
Boy, you're amazing! / by Virginia Kroll ; illustrated by Sachiko Yoshikawa.
p. cm.
Summary: Rhyming text celebrates the many things that boys can achieve.
ISBN 0-8075-0868-3 (hardcover)
[1. Conduct of life--Fiction. 2. Stories in rhyme.] I. Title: Boy, you are amazing!
II. Yoshikawa, Sachiko, ill. III. Title.
PZ8.3.K8997Bo 2004   [E]--dc22   2003018715

The design is by Carol Gildar.

For more information about Albert Whitman & Company,
visit our web site at www.albertwhitman.com.

Boy, you're amazing, the things you can do!

Cut out a birthday card, write "I love you,"

build a snow fort and tell time on the clock,

ride your big bike all the way down the block.

Boy, you're amazing; watch how you play!
A crazy eights card game that lasts the whole day,

firefighter, castle knight in pretend fights,

fast flashlight-tagger
on warm summer nights.

Boy, you're amazing, the things that you know!
How to grow flowers, and signing "hello,"

when to feed Purry, and how to brush Max,
where to hit notes on your new brassy sax.

Boy, you're amazing, the things you create!

Outer space mobiles, a map of your state,

comic strips, web pages, songs of your own,

a sprinkled, two-flavored, three-scoop ice-cream cone.

Boy, you're amazing; just look how you give!

Setting those fireflies free so they'll live;

adding a coat to the "Warm the Kids" box,

loaning your sister your best soccer socks.

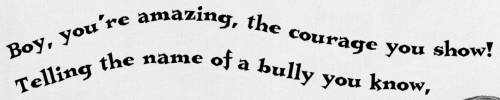

Boy, you're amazing, the courage you show!
Telling the name of a bully you know,

confessing to Grandma you broke her best cup,

staying calm when a storm wakes Baby up.

Boy, you're amazing; wow, look at you go!
Blading on pavement or boarding in snow,

Pitching a no-hitter (hey, what an aim!),

shaking the winning team's hands
with "good game."

Boy, you're amazing and, oh, what a friend!

Saying "I'm sorry" so hurt feelings mend,

raking for Jake, helping Pam write her poem,

making the new kid feel quickly at home.

Boy, you're amazing; hey, look what you are!
Spelling champ, bird-feeder, talent show star,

paper boy, Scout, "Read-to-Me" volunteer,

pet shelter pal, model train engineer,

son, grandchild, brother,

and great cousin, too—

think of the things you will grow up to do!

Dave, Seth, Josh, Noah, Nate, Jeremy, Jim,
Mike, Malik, Ethan, Quinn, Zack, Hunter, Tim,
Jeff, Theo, Ben, Ed, Karim, Liam, Jess,
Tom, Ty, Walt, Chris, Logan, Yoshi, Joe, Wes,
Mark, Andrew, Matt, Ebong, Aaron, Ken, John,
Ravi, Rob, Sam, Cody, Nick, Neil, Don,

Steve, Caleb, Hector, Hans, Abe, Eric, Stan,
Cam, Justin, Luke, Jason, Chase, Adam, Dan,
Brad, Brian, Gabe, Gary, Blake, Harry, Will,
Chad, Charlie, Patrick, Paul, Chee, Devin, Phil,
Peter, Sean, Vince, Carlos, Kev, Ivan, Lou...

Boy, you're amazing!
I'm glad that
you're YOU!